Grammy really loves you,
that's no lie...

More than a birdie,
way up in the sky.

More than a cow
eating grass up on a hill,

or a silly shark chef,
cooking dinner on the grill!

More than a turtle
running in a race...

or a blue and yellow fishy
with a smile on his face!

More than a kitty cat
singing a song...

or a cute little fly
that is buzzing right along!

More than a rhino with an ice cream cone...

or a doggy that is chewing on a great, big bone!

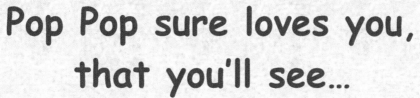

Pop Pop sure loves you,
that you'll see...

more than a piggy
surfing on the sea!

More than an octopus
wearing a hat...

or a red and black tie
on a big, fat cat!

More than a super-pig
flying in the sky...

or a crazy caterpillar
with some great, big eyes!

More than a chickie,
sitting in the sun...

or a whale in the ocean,
having FUN! FUN! FUN!

More than the sunshine
in the sky above...

or a couple little duckies
that are falling in love!

When the stars shine bright...

or the sky is blue...

Grammy really loves you...

Pop Pop loves you too!

Grammy and Pop Pop Love You by Sally Helmick North

Sally was born in Jackson, Michigan. She has lived all over the country with her husband, Fred. They have 3 grown children. She has written over 30 children's books and had her first book published in 2000. Sneaky Snail Stories are all sweet and simple rhyming books with really cute illustrations. You can see all the Sneaky Snail Stories at: www.sneakysnailstories.com

Other books by Sally:
Grandma and Grandpa Love You! (Many versions)
Mimi Loves You! (Many versions)
I Love Noah! (Many names available)
I Love Emma! (Many names available)
Noah Loves Animals (Many names available)
Emma Loves Animals (Many names available)

Search Amazon for "Personalized book for (child's name) by Sally Helmick North"
Or visit my website: www.kidsbookwithname.com

Made in the USA
Monee, IL
10 March 2023